The Velveteen Rabbit

Retold by **Harriet Winfield** Illustrated by **José Miralles**

SRA McGraw-Hill

Columbus, Ohio

A Division of The McGraw·Hill Companies

SRA/McGraw-Hill

A Division of The **McGraw·Hill** Companies

Printed in the United States of America.

Send all inquiries to:
SRA/McGraw–Hill
250 Old Wilson Bridge Road
Suite 310
Worthington, OH 43085

0-02-674641-7

1 2 3 4 5 6 7 8 9 BUX 01 00 99 98 97

Timmy was a little boy who had lots of toys, and he liked to play with all of them. But his favorite toy was the velveteen rabbit that he received on his fourth birthday. Oh, how he loved that soft cuddly rabbit. At night, he could not go to sleep unless he snuggled up with the rabbit close to his body. When he played out in the yard, he always had that rabbit with him. He even talked to his velveteen rabbit.

After a while, the rabbit started to show signs of wear. It became tattered and torn. One of its ears no longer stood up. And its color had changed from a pretty pink color to gray. But Timmy loved it even more than when he had first held it.

Timmy's mother tried to interest Timmy in other toys. She wanted to get rid of the velveteen rabbit because she thought it was dirty and ugly. She said, "Why don't you give me the rabbit, and I'll get you a fine new animal to play with."

"No," Timmy said. "This rabbit is not like the others. This rabbit is real."

"Real?" his mother said. "He's just a toy."

"No," Timmy insisted. "He's real."

The next day, Timmy was playing with the tattered rabbit in the yard when it started to rain. Timmy went inside, but he forgot to take the rabbit with him. When it was time for Timmy to go to bed, he remembered where the rabbit was. He snuck outside in the rain and cold and searched for the rabbit until he found it. Then he hugged his rabbit and said, "You are cold and wet, but I will make you feel better." He took the rabbit inside, dried it, and took it to bed with him. He snuggled up and went to sleep.

A few days later, Timmy became very sick. He had a high fever and strange dreams. In one of his dreams a lovely princess appeared. She said, "The love your rabbit has for you will make you well. And your love for the rabbit will make him real."

Timmy got well, and he remembered what the princess had said. But as the months passed, the poor rabbit became even shabbier than it had been. Part of its stuffing was coming out, and it had a large rip on its back.

One day, Timmy's mother said, "Timmy, you are a big boy now. It's time for you to get rid of that rabbit. It's falling apart."

Timmy said, "But a princess told me that this rabbit will become a real rabbit."

His mother said, "Then why don't you take him out into the woods and leave him there, where he can live with the other rabbits."

Sadly, Timmy agreed. With tears in his eyes, he took his tattered velveteen rabbit to the woods. He put it down in soft leaves, next to a large tree. He patted it and said, "I . . . I have to leave you here . . . but you will be fine . . . . You will be a real rabbit."

He started to walk away, but after he took a few steps he turned around to look at his rabbit for the last time. To his surprise, the tattered rabbit was gone. And sitting in its place was a bunny— a real rabbit.

The bunny hopped over to Timmy and seemed to smile. "Oh," Timmy cried. "You are real." Then the bunny hopped over to where two other bunnies were playing. They welcomed their new friend, and the three of them hopped off.

Timmy often went back into the woods to watch his bunny play with the other rabbits. Although it had changed, Timmy knew that his velveteen rabbit would always love him as much as he loved it.